Tortoise! Tortoise!

Story by Jane Langford
Pictures by Andy Peters

OXFORD
UNIVERSITY PRESS

Tortoise was asleep in his shell.

Zzzz! Zzzz!

3

4

Tortoise woke up.
"Can I come out of my shell today?" said Tortoise.

"No, don't come out today," said Squirrel. "It's very windy! It's autumn."

6

"Can I come out of my shell now?" said Tortoise.

8

"No, don't come out now," said Robin. "It's too cold. It's winter!"

"Can I come out yet?" said Tortoise.

"No, not yet!" said Frog, "It's a very wet spring day!"

11

13

"Why?" said Tortoise.

16